Balzer + Bray is an imprint of HarperCollins Publishers.

Fox and the Jumping Contest
Copyright © 2016 by Corey R. Tabor
All rights reserved. Manufactured in China.
No part of this book may be used or reproduced in any manner whatsoever without
written permission except in the case of brief quotations embodied in critical articles
and reviews. For information address HarperCollins Children's Books, a division of
HarperCollins Publishers, 195 Broadway, New York, NY 10007.
www.harpercollinschildrens.com

ISBN 978-0-06-239874-1

The artist used pencil, watercolor, colored pencil, and ink, assembled digitally, to
create the illustrations for this book.
Typography by Dana Fritts
16 17 18 19 20   SCP   10 9 8 7 6 5 4 3 2 1
❖
First Edition

For Mandy

The jumping contest was only a few days away, and Fox was determined to win first prize. He would put the trophy right there, just above the fireplace.

While the other animals practiced, Fox schemed.
(When you're a fox, every contest is a scheming contest.)

"Aha," said Fox. "I know just the thing."

He built a jetpack and painted it to match his fur so
nobody would notice.

At last, it was the day of the jumping contest. The judges were ready. The animals stretched until they were properly stretchy.

Frog jumped first. He got extra points for style.

Turtle did better than expected.

Elephant couldn't jump at all, but she didn't mind. She was good at other things.

Bear jumped loudest.

Then it was Rabbit's turn.

Fox was last. He took a deep breath. He lifted a paw to test the wind. He wiggled his tail, closed his eyes, and . . .

jumped.

"Winner!" shouted
the animals. "Bravo!"

But where did Fox go?

Oh, there he was.

His scheme had worked too well
and he'd jumped a little too high.

Luckily, Fox never left home without
his emergency inflatable space helmet.

Unluckily, he'd forgotten a parachute.

Meanwhile, the animals were still searching for Fox.

But he was nowhere to be found. They would just have to start the awards ceremony without him.

The judges gave Elephant fifth place, but she didn't mind. Five was her favorite number, and fifth was her favorite place.

Turtle got fourth place for exceeding expectations.

Frog was awarded third place for Best High-Flying Non-Musical Dramatic Performance by an Amphibian.

Bear got second place. (The judges were scared to give him anything less.)

And then:

"Girls and boys, ladies and gentlemen, mammals and birds, amphibians, reptiles, and pachyderms, first prize goes to . . ."

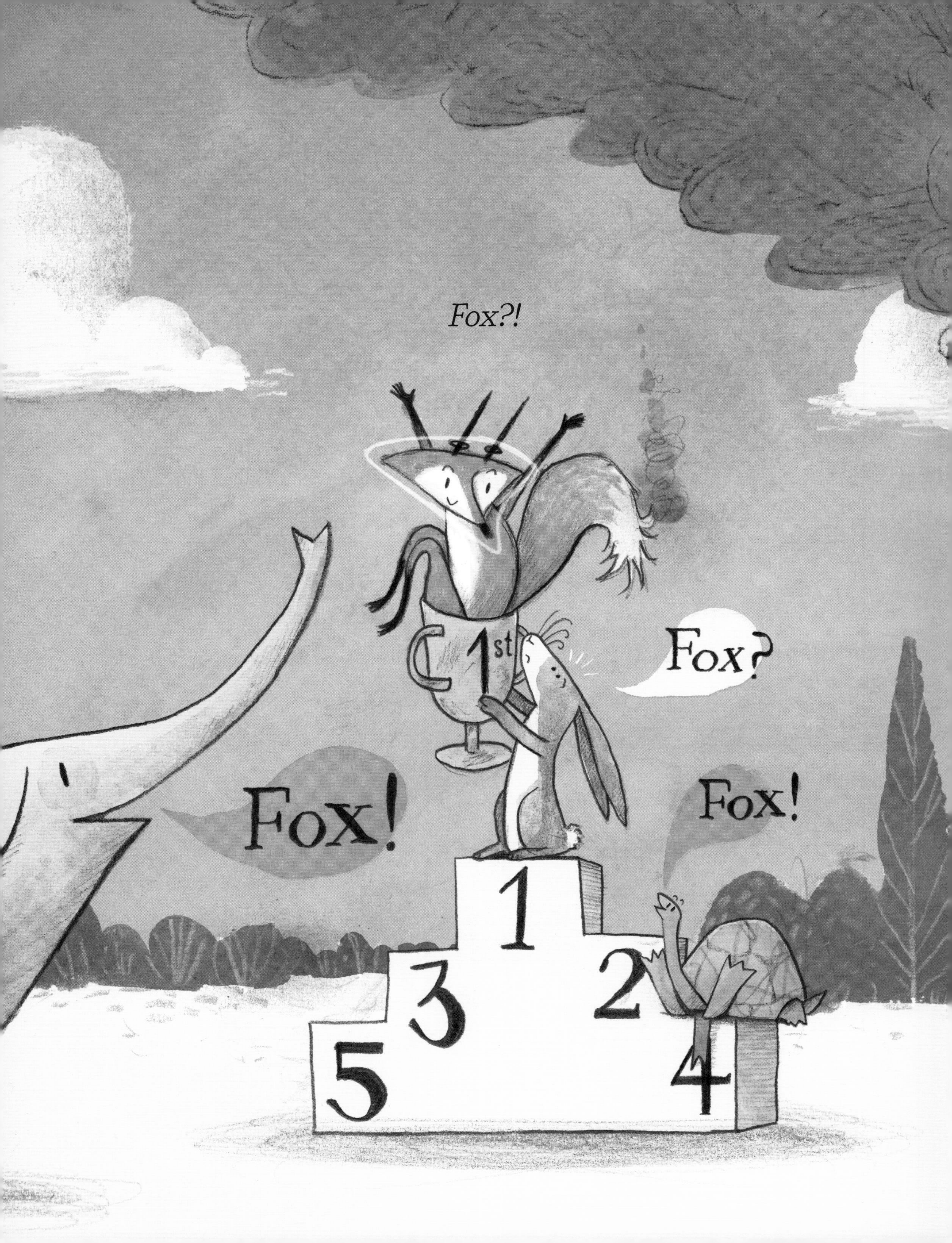
Fox?!
Fox?
Fox!
Fox!
1st
1
2
3
4
5

The trophy fit right there, just above the
fireplace. Fox smiled. Now, if only he could
remember where he'd left his jetpack. . . .